MURMURS

by

Carol Battaglia

Edited by Carolyn S. Zagury, MS, RN, CPC

Cover Design and Original Art Work by Thomas Taylor of Thomcatt Graphics

Vista Publishing, Inc.
473 Broadway
Long Branch, NJ 07740
(908) 229-6500

This publication is designed for the reading pleasure of the general public. All poetry and short stories are the original work of the author.

Printed and bound in the United States of America

First Edition

ISBN: 1-880254-36-0

Library of Congress Catalog Card Number :96-60060

U.S.A. Price $12.95
Canada Price $18.95

DEDICATION

This book is dedicated to the Great Spirit who gave me a soul to hear the murmurs of life, and a voice to speak,

To my husband, Jack, who gave me strength, and love,

To my wonderful teachers at Loyola University Chicago: Mary Ann, Judy and Marianne who encouraged me,

To my dear friends who nurtured me and made me laugh,

And to my mother and her mother who never had the chance to hear my woman's voice.

Thank you one and all.

We are islands whose
boundaries are defined by the
flow of the water around us.

Carol Battaglia
4/8/93

SPECIAL THANKS

I would like to extend my deepest gratitude to Marylin Dalton, of the Towering House Clan, and to her husband Mick, who offered me friendship and a glimpse into Navajo life. And also to all the strong women of the Indian Health Service who took care of me that winter of 1993. I shall never forget your kindness.

Special thanks to Genevive Napier for her technical assistance, and to Carol Lazzarotto for her help in first showing me how to display my poems.

And lastly, to Carolyn Zagury and the people at Vista Publishing, thank you for having faith in me and for giving me this opportunity to show my work.

If in our lives we are blessed
with the gift of a dream come true,
then we must remember all those who
gave us the peace to sleep and
hence to dream.

Carol Battaglia

MEET THE AUTHOR

Carol Battaglia is a nurse at Loyola University Medical Center in Maywood, Illinois.

When asked about her writing she says that she prefers to call it "proetry," a mixture of prose and poetry. She is aware that her poems step outside the boundaries that define the classical structure of what a poem should look like. But Carol is quick to remark that ....

"*we all capture and record the rhythms of life in our own personal way.*"

Carol and her husband Jack enjoy hiking in the canyons around Sedona, Arizona. The picture on this page was taken in one of her favorite places adjacent to the Enchantment Resort at the mouth of Boynton Canyon.

TABLE OF CONTENTS

TABLE OF CONTENTS

TRAPPED

Each of us carries a poem inside.
Some personal rhythm that sways within.
Some cadence that is our own.
Some secret that sings unknown.
Often abandoned and left unheard,
its fate is sealed with ours
eternally interred.

BONDAGE

Babbling voices
of women bound,
by the silent
tongues of men.

FREE

I have been puzzled by the words,
wondering where they were before.
Wondering what kept them down, what
hid them from me. As they appear
now and spill over the page, I
marvel at the feeling behind them
and wonder how I ever held them
captive. They are more me than
I am, and I am glad that their
release has set me free.

EMERGENCE

Climbing the mountain
of my 49th year, my
step falters.

Frightened by the
prospect of what lies
ahead I hold back,
attempting to stave
off the burden of time.

I dress myself with the
cloth of girl hood dreams
and ignore the tightness
of the fit.

Painted by time, shaped
by experience, I no
longer recognize myself.

Dancing inside of me
is the promise of wisdom,
of peace, rhythmically
urging me forward, guiding
my step.

I attempt to follow their
lead, but stand frozen with
the fear of growing old.

I search surrounding faces
for some hint of who I
have become, some image
with which I can live.

Definition eludes me,
and so I begin again.

Climbing the mountain
of my 49th year,
I evolve.

UNION

I wade through family ghosts
        and find,
the essence of who they were
        molding me.

Brushed by shadowless souls
        I crystallize,
a fusion of ethereal legacy
        and self.

SPIRIT OF THE CANYON

The old Indian sensed her presence before actually seeing her. He felt a break in the rhythm of the canyon stillness and knew that he was no longer alone. He heard her then, nosily tramping on the narrow path, and decided that the sounds were human. As he watched her climb the rocks toward his praying place, he wondered why the white woman was alone in this canyon, miles from the main road.

He studied her ascent, observing that most anglos walked on the earth without being part of the rocks or clay or dirt. He knew this to be their way, but it still puzzled him. Are their feet not able to feel their mother's body, does not their skin know the feel of her breath, the wind? He thought about these things as he followed her upward climb.

She was getting closer now and he recognized the smell of fear that she carried with her. She had not seen him yet, being too busy negotiating the rocky climb. She stopped for a minute to catch her breath and clung to the cliff wall like a spider. She interested him. He wanted to know her story and the story of her fear and of her climb. She was almost upon him now, he did not move a muscle for fear that it would startle her. Their eyes met, joining their spirits for one brief second before she screamed. He smiled and held out his hand which she gratefully accepted. He helped her over the cliff edge and watched as she collapsed with relief at his side.

"You gave me quite a scare," she said. He nodded and smiled again hoping to lessen her fear. "I did not expect to find anyone up here. I have been climbing for 2 hours, not really sure of where I was going. I made a wrong turn sometime this morning and kind-of got lost," she said.

He waited for her to finish, not wanting to be impolite and interrupt her conversation. He was an old man and accustomed to the chatter of women. He learned early in life that women often spoke what they were thinking and that it did not pay to intrude until they were emptied of their thoughts.

"What are you doing here? Have you been here long? Are you lost?" She should be finished soon, he thought. So far he had not spoken one word to this stranger.

She seemed quieter now, her breathing more even and relaxed. She looked him over curiously, wondering if he was deaf, or if he understood her. She pulled a pack of cigarettes from her pocket and offered one to the old man.

He accepted her offering, not wanting to tell her that he did not smoke. He placed the gift between weather worn lips and nodded a sign of thanks. She lit hers and watched the smoke disappear into the thin air of the canyon, like incense in a church.

They sat for a while in silence, neither thinking it strange that something or someone had brought them together. She glanced over at the old man and watched the repetitive movement of his lips, wondering if he was praying, she turned away. She had never been in a canyon, and she had certainly never sat beside an old silent Indian man deep in prayer. She felt safe here with him, and less afraid. The cloak of fear she usually wore seemed somehow less heavy.

The old man started to sing, she could not make out the words. They were more sounds than words. The cadence of his music was ancient, it floated into the canyon and disappeared into the air around them. The timbre of his prayer touched her, as if he had actually laid his hands on her. She felt better than she had in a very long time.

He sat there, thinking about her, aware of her trouble. From deep inside him came a song to the Great Mother, for he was a Yavapai, and this was their sacred canyon. But the white woman would not know this, would not understand the holiness of the place that she had wandered into. He would speak to her soon, tell her that he had come here to die.

"You must be wondering what I am doing her," she said. "I came because I was afraid to come, because I am tired of always living in fear. I thought that if I could do something that frightened me I could learn to live again without fear. I came here to learn how to live."

The old man looked into her soul. She had come here to live and he to die. The canyon walls would hold them both and grant, in turn, each their wish. His body had housed his spirit for many years, weary now it sought rest.

The sun began its journey home, coloring the cliffs with paint of red and orange. They leaned against the wall of stone and were warmed by the trapped heat of the day. As the blanket of night fell they thought their separate thoughts and dreamed different dreams. As they slept, the body of the old man died. His spirit soared into the night air and hovered above them.

When morning broke the woman awoke feeling stronger than she could ever remember. She was no longer afraid. She looked over to where the old man had been. He was gone. He must have left during the night, she thought. She prepared to leave and reached for her pack of cigarettes, and thought it strange that she no longer wanted to smoke.

DEACTIVATED

I read an interesting sign as I entered the parking garage this morning. It said that "all employees who failed to have a 1993 decal would be deactivated." I visualized some magic moment during the work day when these employees would suddenly slump to the floor or be frozen in some work-related task, or collapse into heaps on their desks ---------DEACTIVATED!

BURDENS

I like to think of Sisyphus, not
burdened by his rock, but of a
Sisyphus freed, if just briefly,
on his journey down the mountain.
I picture him stretching, arching
his back, upright again, lighter,
savoring his weightlessness. His
punishment, perhaps, was not the
weight of the rock, but rather the
awareness of the lightness without it.

LAMENT

I saw someone troubled today and did
not stop to inquire why.
Harnessed with my own pain, I had no
room to shoulder his, and so I passed him by.

WOMB

I miss the womb. Its comforting walls,
its nurturing fluid, its peaceful silence,
its cloak of darkness. I miss the soothing
rocking of my mother's breath and the feel
of her warmth. It is cold out here and vast.
And I am not sure how long that I can last.

EMMA AND JESSIE

I have tried very hard not to write about Emma and Jessie, but the compelling memory of them has risen and will not be stilled.

I first saw them about one year ago while visiting friends in Scotland, and the recollection of them has haunted me ever since. The site of them touched me so profoundly that it has taken me this long to free them from my memory.

It is a difficult story to start, and so I will begin by giving the reader some sense of the atmosphere in which they were first spotted.

It was March in Aberdeen, and the winds of the gray North Sea swept the city and carried the gulls on currents high above man. Evening was nearing and the fading light made everything look gray. A light mist-like rain was falling, and was pushed sideways from the wind.

I was sitting on a window seat watching, in comfort, the coming of the Aberdeen night, when I noticed a door open across the courtyard of the apartment complex. I waited to see who would be venturing out into the chilly night, but there did not appear to be anyone beyond the door. Then I saw a black Labrador retriever poke its head outside as if testing the night air.

I called to my friend Betty and asked her to whom the dog belonged. “Oh that’s Jessie,” she said. “Watch a minute and you will see her owner, Emma.” Jessie stepped out into the night followed slowly at the end of a thick leash by Emma. Emma was a tall thin youngish woman wrapped in a great gray coat. She walked haltingly and looked a little unsteady. Jessie pulled her into the courtyard and the walk of the night began.

“Emma has Rheumatoid Arthritis,” Betty said. “Jessie is her power.” I watched as they made their way down the winding street. Jessie would stop often granting Emma rest and then they would continue again.

From where I sat I could observe the stiffness of Emma’s gait and I wondered if she was in pain on these nightly walks. “How long has she been ill?” I asked. “For about a year now.” Betty answered. “She used to work in town, but she is gradually becoming weaker and needs more and more rest. We all lend a hand and help out as much as we can, but only Jessie can give her the mobility she misses so much.”

As they disappeared from sight, I found myself not wanting to move, fearful that I would miss their return. I sat waiting and searching the darkened street for any sign of them. Finally I spotted Jessie slowly pressing against the wind, piloting Emma back to safety. I watched as they made their way in to the courtyard, this symbiotic pair, struggling to complete their nightly ritual, connected by more than the leash that held them together.

Nearing the door to their apartment they stopped and turned to face the night, perhaps giving thanks for a safe return. Emma patted Jessie's great black head and Jessie nudged closer as if acknowledging Emma's gratitude. They then entered the building, leaving the night somewhat empty by their absence.

I sat for a while longer, thinking about what I had witnessed, tucking the memory of them deep inside me. The sight of Jessie with her strength and steadiness propelling Emma through the streets of Aberdeen lives inside of me, and at times on cold rainy nights the memory of them emerges and I wonder if they are all right.

My fear is that Emma will weaken and not be able to care for Jessie or that something will happen to Jessie, sentencing Emma to the imprisonment of her infirmity. My hope is that they will survive the coldness of night and gain comfort from each other and from the warmth of the day.

That one brief glimpse of them has somehow connected me to them, I am bound by that memory and find myself obliged to tell their story.

WOLF CRY

I hear the cry of the wolves - -
their ancient music riding on
the high wind speaks to me of
primeval times. The chorus of
their voices, sounding like notes
from muted flutes, surround me.
I wish I knew their language,
could speak their tongue, so
that I might know what message
their song conveys.

EVOLVED

I looked for you today, and you
were nowhere to be found.
I searched all the rooms of my
heart hoping to catch a glimpse
of you in places where you once were bound.
That person that I
had so laboriously erected, so
carefully designed, had fled.
That person now real and no
longer my ideal became liberated
from my hold and survived to
stand alone.

SPRING CLEANING

The spring of my 48th year
was turbulent. Thunderstorms,
lightening, floods and growth,
seemed to mirror my internal climate.

I cleaned incessantly - - tackling closets,
cabinets, and areas of the
house that I had not looked at
in years. I was lost in my
activity - - until I realized that
I was organizing myself.
Straightening the living quarters of self.
Deciding what to keep and
what to shed. Rearranging,
prioritizing, examining aspects of
myself that were hidden and
dusty.

I wore myself out that spring - -
but emerged a little cleaner
and a little less burdened
by what I did not need.

BESIDE YOU

If I could but ease your pain
this very minute, I would.
Free you from this heavy burden,
oh, if only I could. Powerless
I watch and stand beside you.
Silently I wait to catch you
if you fall.

DISTANCE

My mother and I were really never very close - -
for all the reasons that mothers and daughters
over the ages find a gap between them. The
distance shortened as I stood at her casket and
talked with her girlhood friends who told me
stories about the fun-loving girl they knew and
how she made them laugh when they were young.
That gap erected by both of us had kept us from
each other. With a sense of remorse I lamented
the person I never knew - - and I wondered if she
too had these feelings as she laid her mother
to rest.

A PRAYER FOR SLEEP

Lord, I am unable to sleep tonight,
and I seek your comfort.
Unable to shake the grasp of the day
that hangs heavily on me,
I seek your release.
I am tired, Lord, weary.
But my spirit will not rest.
How I long, in my ignorance,
to end this day.
This day which you have given me as a gift.
Instead of valuing each waking moment that
will never be repeated, I seek escape.
How foolish, Lord, how mortal.
Thank You for my wakefulness.

DAWN

I face the east, waiting for
God to lift the sun, and end
the night.

My prayers, riding on the dark
wind, move to meet the day.

The sun presents, the first
miracle of the day in motion.

I retreat, filled with hope
and gratitude.

T. Taylor

EVA

At least once, in most of our lives, we connect with a stranger who happens across our paths and changes our direction, if ever so slightly. The stranger in my life was Eva.

I was vacationing in the canyons of Arizona, thoroughly enjoying the immensity of their peace, when I first met her. I was hiking alone, attempting to master an arduous climb to the Sinaqua ruins several hundred feet above me, when I spotted a woman who appeared to be talking to a cactus. I wiped my eyes not trusting what I was seeing, thinking perhaps that I was delirious from too much sun or that she was one of those mirages that I had heard so much about. But she was still there and still deep in some private conversation with this lonely cactus. She looked to be about fifty, she wore her graying hair in long braids that almost reached her waist. She was dressed completely in black and stood out against the red canyon walls. Her companion, the cactus, was desert green and wore knife-like spines. I strained to hear what she was saying and thought I heard her telling the cactus that she understood how it felt to be alone on the side of a path, isolated from others of its species. "I hope that you are not too lonely," she told the cactus. "For surely there is much to see and enjoy in this beautiful canyon."

At this point, I thought that I had better make myself known to her and to her silent partner, and so I faked a cough and shuffled my feet and pretended to have just arrived. She stood and turned. She smiled cautiously, said "Hello," and introduced herself as "Eva." I fumbled a greeting, conscious of my intrusion into her solitude. As I prepared to pass her on the path, she asked if I was heading up to the ruins. She wondered if she might climb with me. She had apparently attempted the ascent before, but never successfully. I told her that I would be happy to have her company, fully aware of my doubts about my own ability to make the climb. Starting up the trail, I glanced over my shoulder and saw Eva spilling some of her bottled water into the base of the cactus.

We climbed slowly and silently, both needing our concentration for the rocky terrain. After about a half hour we came upon a smooth shelf of red rock and decided to take a break. We sat and talked about the beauty of the canyon and about how we came to be climbing alone. Slowly Eva began to tell me her story. She spoke of her life, and of her fear of growing old. The tale of her life spilled over her lips, and every once in a while she would glance in my direction as if assuring herself that I was still there.

As she talked I thought about how much alike we all really are. Each of us carrying our story inside, needing to hear it told, wanting to give it life, to present it to another, even if the other was a stranger. It is as if in the telling we are validated somehow, made more real. And the cleansing quality of the narrative empties us and makes room for more of life to live. I thought about all these things as Eva spoke. I also thought about the ancient women who once lived in this canyon. I could picture them sitting, perhaps in this very spot, sharing their fears and their hopes. Eva's tale was their tale and my tale and story of all those who would follow us.

Rested, we decided to continue our climb. We looked up at the ruins above us and began the ascent. The steepness of the trail kept us bent, and searching for anything that we could grab on to, Eva said that this climb was just like life, which at times bends us and causes us to struggle in order to reach the top. I agreed, but was too breathless to say so.

Nearing the ruins we felt the cool air from the great cavernous room. It encircled us and drew us toward the opening, like arms pulling us into the body of its chamber. It was a huge half-moon shaped room with a blackened ceiling stained from endless fires, and the only sound that could be heard was the moaning of the wind as it sailed through the crumbling ruin.

I watched Eva as she touched the stone walls. "If only they could speak," she said. "And tell us their secrets, tell us about the people that they have sheltered. Were they so different from us?" She wondered out loud. "Probably not." She answered herself.

I think that she needed to know that, to know that people have always struggled with loneliness and fear, and somehow managed to survive. A thousand years from now people will wonder about us, and perhaps gain some solace from the fact that we endured.

I looked over to where Eva was standing. She appeared to be deep in thought. "Are you all right?" I asked. "I am now." She answered. She said no more.

When I think about that time with Eva, I think about what she might have meant. Did she find something that day? Or did she choose to leave something behind? I will never know. It is unlikely that Eva and I will ever meet again, but I will always remember that climb and the woman named Eva with a story to tell.

IN TOUCH

I felt it again today.
That feeling of being alive.
That feeling that lasts but a
few seconds. That feeling that
connects everything.
That fleeting feeling of harmony.

TO NURSE

To Care
To Solace
To Touch
To Feel
To Hurt
To Need

To Heal, others,
as well as ourselves.

HOSPITAL HALLS

I have walked these hospital halls
for many years now. Thousands of
steps, thousands of words, it's no
wonder I'm tired. Talked out.
The emotions of others swirl around
me. Some happy, some relief, some
burdened with grief. Sometimes I
turn a corner and lose myself,
sometimes I turn a corner and find
myself. You just never know.

REMEMBERING

Sunlight landed on the
bed. The old woman
stretched her fingers
to feel its heat. It
warmed her, it comforted
her, it reminded her of
younger summers . . .
But she could not hold
on and her fingers
slowly slipped into the
shade, as did her life.

FATHER HOGAN

Sleep my brother, rest, agonize no more.
The gods have called you to their door.
Let go, my brother, flee across the threshold.
You will find the longest journey you ever take
involves the shortest step a man can make.
From this world to the next takes but a minute.
A trip often unscheduled, a trip for which
bag and baggage are left behind.

THE SENTENCE

They came to me today and circled my
bed. Not one able to meet my gaze, nor
feel my dread. Their white coats shielding
them from my pain, nothing would ever be
the same again. They told me that I had
cancer, they talked on and on, they did
not even notice that I had left them,
shut down, collapsed within myself.
How short this distance from womb to tomb.

BREATH

I have felt the breath of newborns
sweep softly across my face, and
stood in wonder at the sweetness of
new life.

I have felt the breath of those in
pain, and stood startled as it crashed
jaggedly, hurtfully across my face.
Marking me in its strife.

I have felt the breath of someone
dying, air pulling and tugging at my
face as if trying to capture some of
my life for its own. And I stood
defeated, resigned, and helpless.
Unable to harness its dying force,
unable to stem its flow, I sensed its
final futility and reverently let it go.

THE REUNION
(St. Elizabeth's School of Nursing 1965)

Faces of women,
tiny lines that
verify living.
Glimpses of the
girl behind the
eyes.
Hair, a little
duller, colored
perhaps to girl
hood tones.

Some fatter,
some thinner
with gestures not
seen in 30 years.
Washed by the music
of familiar laughter
the years dissolve.

We, who have been
many things to
many people, gather
together and become
that person that
we once knew.

No pretense, no
apologies, comfortable
with finding ourselves
again, unburdened and
free to be a girl
once more.

Time to leave,
uneasy silence,
donning coats and
present lives we
depart. Stronger
than we arrived.

THE PLIGHT OF NURSING

I am the "Lady with
the lamp."
A stranger moving in
and out of your world
shadow-like.

I brush the edges of your fear,
leaving some of
myself behind.

Sometimes at the
end of my
shift, I cannot
account for all of me.

I retrace my steps,
in hopes of putting
myself back together
again.

THE WORK OF DREAMS

When I awoke, I was lying in a field of high grass. Poor grass, the weight of my fallen body had taken its life. I brushed its broken blades from my face and hair and looked myself over. Everything seemed to be in the right place. Cautiously I moved my arms and legs and was delighted to discover that I was still in one piece. I glanced over to my right and saw a rabbit about ten feet away, staring at me, apparently perplexed at the sight of a grown woman spread eagle on the grassy floor.

I rolled over on my side, spit out some grass, said "Hi" to the rabbit and tried to remember what had happened. "I think I did it this time," I told myself. The memory of those last few moments before the fall slowly coming back to me. I figured that I was only in the air for a few seconds before I crashed, hitting my head and knocking myself out. I could fly! I knew that I had flown. "Did you see me fly?" I asked the rabbit. It just continued to stare at me in its rabbity way. The rabbit had no way of knowing that I have spent the last twenty years of my life trying to fly again, to repeat that first flight so many years ago.

I laid back down on the grassy bed and thought about that first time. I was ten years old, running home from school, pushed by the winds of a breaking storm, trying to make it home before the rains came down. When I realized that my feet were not touching the ground. It frightened me so that I grabbed for the air around me and fell to the ground with a thud! "What the Hell!" I yelled out loud, and then checked around to make sure that no adult was present to hear me say the "H" word. Dazed, I walked slowly home, not caring anymore if the rain came, my ten year old mind not quite grasping the concept of myself in flight. "Maybe I imagined it," I told myself. But I knew that something special had happened. What I did not know was that those first brief moments of flight would change my life forever, and that I would spend my time on earth preoccupied with doing it again.

The next few months in my ten year old life were quite bizarre. I never told anyone what had happened to me, fearing that they would think that I was crazy. I spent my time jumping off stairs, boulders, porches any perch of height that I could find. But nothing happened, I always crashed, flight eluded me. I devised fantastic contraptions to assist me in flight. Once, when rummaging through the attic, I found my dad's old army cap. It was a massive brown leather hat, fleece lined, with huge ear flaps that could be tied under my chin. It was about ten sizes too big for me, but I wore it anyway. I cut a small hole in the top of the cap and inserted a propeller-type thing that I had found on an old beanie. I figured that if it worked for helicopters it might just do the trick for me. I strapped on the cap, climbed up on the family car and jumped off. I nearly killed myself, but I did discover that the old hat cushioned my head from the fall, so I took to wearing the head piece during times of attempted flight.

After that, I noticed that my family was starting to look at me funny, and conversations would often stop when I entered a room. They were worried about me and I saw their relief when I asked if I could have a pet. "A dog would be great," my mother said. "I think that I would rather have a bird, if you don't mind," I replied. I wanted to study the bird, see if I could learn what made it fly. "Well, let's go down to the pet store," my mother relented. "But for goodness sake leave that old hat at home." Reluctantly I did, hoping that no opportunities for flight would present, because I was not sure how much more my head could take.

So, we bought a green parakeet who I named Barney Boy. I spent hours observing him, envious of his flight pattern around our house. But I remained earth bound. Then one day I had what I thought was a great idea, that kind of went sour. I put on an old tight sweatshirt, smeared it with large amounts of paste, broke open a feather pillow and spilled the feathers on the shirt. I can still remember Barney Boy's beady eyes watching me in parakeet disbelief, his pinpoint eyes riveted to my bird shirt. Then I strapped on my trusty leather cap, climbed up on the window sill and leaped out the first floor window. Splat! I landed on my mother's flower bed. Unfortunately, my mother was working on her flowers at the time, and kind-of got crushed. Most of me apparently landed on her head, pushing her face into the hard dirt resulting in a broken nose for my dear mother. I called her "the beak" after that, although never to her face.

Well, that was that. She said that she "had had it!" She just "could not take it anymore," she told me in a nasally tone. It was "off to summer camp for me," she spurted. Where she hoped that "I would be like other little girls, and play with dolls, and have tea parties."

"Fat chance," I said to myself. But I permitted myself to be bundled off to camp, after saying good-bye to a smug Barney Boy and packing my leather cap.

The stiffness of my limbs recalled me from my memories. I sat up and noticed that the rabbit was still in attendance, and that it did not appear to be frightened by my movement. I thought this strange, but I liked its company. "Let's move to the shade of that tree," I told the rabbit. Great, I thought, now I am talking to a rabbit as well as trying to fly. The guys in white coats with nets should arrive at any minute, I warned myself.

I stood and stretched, my bruised muscles rebelling against the movement. As I limped over to the enticing shade, I caught site of the rabbit cautiously following me. I planted myself against the trunk of the tree and felt refreshed in its shadow. The rabbit rested at the edge of the shade margin and rhythmically wrinkled its nose.

I closed my eyes and thought about my life and about my obsession with flight. Perhaps it was time to give up the dream, to face the reality of being rooted to this earth.

I thought about all those times the dream had held me, the hope of it acting as a buffer against an encroaching world. It was that hope that brought me to this field of grass for one last attempt. I told myself that if I did not succeed this time I would fold the dream away and get on with my life.

So, what did happen before the fall? The effort of remembering made my head ache, but I seemed to recall running very fast and leaping into the air. What happened after that only the rabbit knew and he was not telling.

Perhaps its better not to know, I cautioned myself. Maybe I need the delusion. But deep inside of me I knew that people could not really fly, that it was absurd to believe that the laws of nature would bend and release me from gravity's hold.

"Time to face reality," I told the rabbit. "We two must walk or hop, as the case maybe, grounded and bound to this earth." Surprisingly the rabbit inched closer, as if understanding that he was witnessing the release of a hope long harbored.

"Humans need their dreams," I advised him. "It is what gets us through the dark of night, and through the troubled times of light. We need to hang on to something. We search our lives for some sign, some evidence that these dreams are possible and that they might come true and rescue us from our ordered lives."

Weary now and somewhat saddened at the prospect of relinquishing my own dream, I watched the rabbit turn and head toward the field of grass. I did not blame him for his abandonment of me. He had proven himself a good companion, generous with his time and a good listener.

He began to run. Faster and faster he went, until his legs no longer touched the ground. And then, he just flew away!

FOR SARAH, OF THE HOMELESS

They walk, heeding
some hidden rhythm,
isolated from others,
worn from pressing
against voices of
past lives.

Like angels cast
from paradise, they
seek refuge.

They move among us.
We dare not meet
their gaze. The
price too high.

OBSERVATION IN CHILD ABUSE COURT

I can barely recognize the
emotion, it is what comes
after misery, it is further
than dispair, it hangs
suspended in the air, it
moves around the room
bouncing against us,
it is foreign, we will
never know it, it is not
of us. It has no way out,
it feeds itself, it will
be willed to the children
of the children and to their
children and to their children.
Until it wears itself out.

MAKING IT

Don't you just feel like a squirrel
sometimes, trying to cross a busy road.
Sensing the vibrations of what is coming
and trying not to get hit.
Happy to make it to the other side.

UNEXPRESSED

You cannot push a poem.
Either its there or its not.
You cannot find it within yourself
if it does not want to be found.
It hides skillfully in depths
unreachable.
It is the song of the soul, the
painting of self, the very music
of life around you.
But sometimes it escapes expression
and you are left with an internal
fullness that strains your boundaries
until you think that you will burst.

MINISTRATIONS

Born in the midst of strangers,
lifted from my mother's womb, skin
washed, eyes opened and cleansed,
they prepared me to meet my first
day. And gently cradled me in my
mother's arms.

Death in the midst of strangers,
lifted from my earthly place.
Skin washed, eyes closed by unknown
hands, they prepared me for my last
day. And gently placed me in mother
earth.

What irony that this so intimate of
care is delivered by strangers, with
faces unseen by me.

THE MESSAGE IN MEMORIES

Its funny how the memories of childhood flow episodically through our lives. Something triggers their return and we find ourselves wrapped in incidences of the past like some kind of time travelers.

Today, for some reason, I was thinking about my Aunt Barb and Uncle Bud. They were wonderful characters. They were the complete opposites of each other and lived in the most dysfunctional house that I have ever seen.

Aunt Barb was a cross between Donna Reed and June Ward. She wore shirtwaist dresses accessorized with an old string of pearls while cleaning the house.

Bud, her husband, always appeared somewhat disheveled. He went through life looking as if he just woke up from a long sleep. He had this coin collection that he would work on for hours at a time. Bud sat slumped over the coins that were scattered on the dining room table. He wore a green visor, an old tee shirt and crumpled pants.

My aunt loved Bud very much, and dusted around him singing old show tunes. She waltzed through the house as if it were a palace. She seemed not to mind that most everything was broken or just simply askew.

Aunt Barb kept long lists for Bud of the things that needed to be fixed. I thought it hilarious that even the lists looked like they needed to be mended. Sometimes torn or stained they hung on a warped bulletin board in the kitchen.

On his way to the stove for a cup of coffee, Uncle Bud would stop to review the lists, sometimes adding an item with a broken pen held together with a rubber band. He'd stand there, his big hand wrapped around a coffee mug, and tell my aunt that he would have to get busy and start on the repairs. "Good idea, Hon," my aunt would reply as she continued her dance with the dust.

Now in this house lived a small menagerie of handicapped animals. There was Buster, the deaf bull dog, a stocky good natured dog who kind of resembled Uncle Bud. He was "deaf as a door nail" as Bud liked to say, but sensitive to the slightest of vibrations. Buster circled the house every half-hour or so, stopping at my uncle and aunt for a friendly pat on his massive head. On his back he often carried the family parakeet Ernie who could not fly.

They kept Ernie's cage on an old chair in the corner of the kitchen. On his trips around the house Buster would stand beside the cage and Ernie would climb on Buster's back like some passenger boarding a scheduled bus. Buster would then deposit Ernie at various spots around the house. Ernie's favorite place was the window seat in the living room where he would sit and watch the birds outside and occasionally flutter his wings.

Sometimes Buster would carry Ernie to the dining room table and Ernie would walk among Uncle Bud's coins, or peck at my uncle's finger signaling that he wanted to be lifted to the green visor. Nestled there, he appeared to be inspecting the coins. It was really a sight to behold.

There was also a cat in the house named Mamie. She was a white ball of fur and only had one eye. It was the bluest of blue, and she reminded you of a white cloud with a spot of blue sky peaking through. No one found it strange that my aunt and uncle had picked her out of twenty strays at the animal shelter.

Mamie loved Aunt Barb, and in those rare moments when my aunt was not dusting or making fix-it lists, Mamie would sit on her lap and swipe at the pearls around her neck. When my aunt was busy, Mamie would follow Buster around waiting for him to rest. She would then squeeze herself under his great chin and take a nap. Buster did not seem to mind, and when you caught them sleeping it looked as if Buster was resting his head on a soft white pillow.

I loved to stop at my aunt and uncle's on my way home from school. The peaceful disarray was soothing. Uncle Bud had found a pink visor for me at a garage sale, and we would sit, capped, examining the coins like some members of an exclusive club. Much of the geography and history I remember today I learned from Uncle Bud.

One day in to this homey chaos there came a stranger. He presented himself at the half-door in the kitchen. Now most doors of this type were kept closed at the bottom and the top half swung open. But in their kitchen the top part of the door was stuck and the lower half was opened.

We heard a knock on the door, and Aunt Barb and I followed Buster into the kitchen to see who was there. What we saw was the bottom half of a man on crutches with only one leg. He spoke into the door saying that he was looking for work and did we have anything that needed "fixin."

Well, even as a kid, I knew that this guy had hit the mother load. Aunt Barb asked him to wait and called for Uncle Bud. He appeared wearing his visor and Ernie. She told him what the man wanted. There was a moment of silence as we stared at the bottom half of the man and watched Buster sniff his single leg and then wag his stubby tail.

My uncle, trusting Buster's judgment, asked the man in. This cntailcd some maneuvering as the man balanced himself on his crutches while ducking under the door. Once inside he looked us over and pronouncing us safe agreed to sit and have a cup of coffee.

He was a slim man with the kind of face that made you think that he had seen much, and perhaps more than he ever wanted. He looked to be about the same age as my uncle, but seemed more worn. As if he somehow got used up along the way. He wore faded jeans, a black tee shirt and carried a beat up back pack. His dark hair was pulled back in a pony tail.

He said his name was Archie and that he was a Viet Nam vet and that was where he had lost his leg. He asked my aunt and uncle if they had any odd jobs. He said that he could fix most anything and would be willing to do so for a small price and meals.

Aunt Barb looked at my uncle. Ernie and Uncle Bud were staring at the bulletin board that hung crookedly on the kitchen wall. "Well, we might have a few things for you to do," my uncle said. "When could you start?"

"I could be here in the morning," Archie replied.

"Sounds good to me," Uncle Bud said. "See you at breakfast."

We watched as Archie made his way under the door and down the street. Uncle Bud transferred Ernie to Buster's back and they resumed their daily rounds.

So, Archie showed up that next day and the day after that. And the days moved to weeks and then to months. Archie fixed up the room over the garage, moved in and became part of the household.

He did not talk much at first, he just went about his business meticulously repairing the broken things in the house. As time passed he told us about how he had lost his leg in the last days of the war and about how he could not find work when he returned home. "It seemed," he said, "that no one had much use for a one-legged carpenter."

I remember thinking back then, that people could break and that they were harder to mend. Because no one could really fix another person. That healing had to come from inside, and that this was a slow process as people somehow reorganized themselves and got on with their lives.

As an adult, I have grown to understand that Archie was somehow broken inside, but could fix anything on the outside. And that my aunt and uncle were complete on the inside, but could not repair anything on the outside. Some trick of fate, some game of the gods had brought these people together, and had given them as gifts to each other.

I am thinking about all of this as I look at their picture pinned to the bulletin board that slopes unevenly over my desk. It was taken in the kitchen and shows Uncle Bud wearing his green visor. Standing next to him is my aunt neatly dressed and next to her is Archie with a hint of a smile on his face. He is holding up a broken crutch, and in some strange way, I know that this means he is healing. Buster is at their feet with Ernie balanced on his head. The cat Mamie is sitting in the space made vacant by Archie's missing leg.

As I said at the beginning, its funny how memories reappear. Once recalled, for that brief moment, they have within them a message whose power never really quite diminishes.

TINSEL

Someone asked me once to describe something that
I had seen that made me smile, that made me
happy. I thought for a while - - and then I remembered
a discarded robin's nest that I had found last
summer. I picked it up because something shiny
caught my eye. As I marveled at its complicated
construction, I saw a piece of Christmas tinsel
woven into its walls. That tinsel which had
graced someone's tree had witnessed the birth of
baby birds. That really made me smile. I kept
it a while, but then freed it to do other work.

MEDIOCRITY

Well into my forties,
I choose not to say how far.
I am faced with the reality of
my mediocrity.
Being not the worst, nor the best.
Not the slimmest, nor the fattest.
Not ugly, but not quite pretty.
I take inventory of myself and
grapple with what I find.

I know instinctively that in order
to survive, I must accept what I
discover. Must cease yearning for
what I do not possess. Must stop
fashioning some mythical model of
woman designed in childhood,
patterned after I know not whom.
Quit chasing unlived dreams, and
listening for cries of those unborn.

Confronted with this my reality, I strive
to regard myself with kindness.
I have lived, after all, these
forty some years, without hurting
many, or causing much sorrow.
I have given some joy, made a few
people laugh and held the hands of
strangers.

THE CROSSING

Crossing a busy street
I saw an older woman
stop and grasp the arm
of her daughter, protecting
her from traffic's flow.

I thought about all those
times that my mother did
that to me. And about
how it irritated me so,
and about how embarrassing
it was, and about how I
brushed her hand away.

But today, I long for the
touch of her arm on mine.
I miss you Mom!

GIFTS

I have my father's nose
and my mother's heart.
And, at times, I ponder
the largeness of each gift.

I AM MY MOTHER'S DAUGHTER

I am my
Mother's daughter,
though fighting it
these many years.

I glimpse her
look in morning
mirrors, assessing
who I have become.

I catch my
hand in her gestures,
I hear her sneak into my laugh.

I am myself,
but she.
I am her mother
and her mother's
mother.

And the magic of
the umbilical cord
softly links us all.

I am my mother's
daughter, with this
one great grief.
That I have lost
the chance, my only
chance, to find
myself in her.

SAMS
SAMS
Chili

BENT WOMAN AND FAT SAM

Her Navajo name was Adzaan Ya-shi-yizh, anglo translation, "Bent Woman." She was known to be a spirit tracker, and people sought her wisdom hoping that she might help them find that part of themselves that they had lost.

Bent since childhood, she spent her time on earth perpetually bowed. Her people said that was why she could track the escaping spirits. They said the spirit struggled to leave the body and left marks upon the ground, but Bent Woman never said this was so, because she would not talk about the spirits.

No one knew for sure how old she was. She looked ancient, but her face, though wrinkled, was soft. It had been sheltered these many years by her bent position, which shielded her from the desert sun. She wore her hair pulled back and knotted in the traditional Navajo way. Her long skirt brushed the ground and she always seemed to be surrounded by a fine cloud of dust.

Bent Woman lived in a traditional Hogan with her daughter and granddaughter in the hills outside of Gallup, New Mexico. Their camp was a steady two mile climb from the main road over mud-packed terrain, that the Bureau of Indian Affairs humorously called a road.

I first heard about Bent Woman from my mother, who learned of her while working on the reservation. My mother told me many stories about her life among the Navajos. She admired their gentleness and resilience, their love for the land, their acceptance of the natural way, and their quest for "ho-zho-go," a way of living in harmony with everything around them.

Being a city girl, I did not understand all that she said, but I loved to hear her speak of Bent Woman and the power she possessed to mend people broken by the troubles of life.

My favorite story, the one I had my mother tell me over and over again, was about Bent Woman and Fat Sam. Fat Sam was a three hundred pound Mexican who lived around Gallup. Fat Sam loved to eat, and would devour huge amounts of fry bread laced with honey every day. He ran a diner just outside of town, and people came from miles around to eat his famous chili and share a laugh and gossip with the big man. Sam was known for his generosity, he often would feed people down on their luck with only a promise of payment when things got better.

People felt comfortable at Sam's and gathered there to exchange reservation news. They liked to watch Sam squeeze himself down the narrow aisle behind the diner counter. They joked that one day he would become wedged and have to be pried loose. Sam did not mind these jokes because he loved his diner and enjoyed the stories of his customers.

Then early one morning, as he was making his chili and egg specialty, two women appeared framed in the patched screen door. As Sam looked closer he saw a small girl tucked behind the younger woman. The older woman was bent from the waist and studied the ground. "Yaa'eh t'eeh," the young woman said. "Ya teeh," Sam responded. The woman asked if he could spare some water, she said they had traveled down from the hills to do some business in Gallup. He welcomed them in and set up three glasses of cold water on the diner counter. They drank slowly, the small girl sneaking glances at Sam, the biggest man that she had ever seen. He wondered if the women were hungry, but he did not want to embarrass them with an offer of food in case they did not have the money to pay for the meal. "Do you think you could do me a favor?" he asked the women. "I just made some chili, but I think it is too salty. I would be grateful if you would try it and tell me what you think." The young girl looked at the middle woman, who in turn whispered to the bent woman and then listened to her reply.

"We could do that," she said. Sam set up three bowls of chili, topped them each with a poached egg and served a biscuit on the side. He poured the women some coffee and set a glass of milk next to the young girl's dish. The woman and the girl waited for Bent Woman to begin eating and then they followed. They ate in silence, seemingly testing the chili for too much salt. When they finished they talked among themselves and then called Sam over. "We think the chili is very good," said the middle woman. "And we thank you for letting us try it."

Sam gathered up their bowls and crammed his way down the aisle over to the sink. He looked up into the mirror above the sink and saw the bent woman whisper something to her daughter. "My mother would like to repay your kindness of the breakfast," the woman said.

"Don't mention it," Sam replied. But he was curious about what the old woman could possible offer.

Bent Woman spoke in rhythmic Navajo, and the young girl slid off the diner stool and went to stand beside her. She listened attentively and every once and a while glanced up at Fat Sam and nodded her head. "My grandmother says that you have a sister," the young one said. "And that this woman is sick with sadness."

Startled, Sam stopped washing the bowls. For he did indeed have a sister, whom he loved dearly. His sister had become as thin as Sam was fat, and in his simple life she was the one heartache that he owned.

"Grandmother says that the sad woman has lost her will to live, that all joy has left her."

Tears welled up in Sam's eyes, because this was true. Ever since the death of her baby two months ago his sister had grieved herself into a space of sadness that she could not be recalled from.

The old woman spoke again saying, through her granddaughter, that the sad woman was holding the spirit of her dead baby to earth. That this act of not letting go had cost Sad Woman's grief to build. She must free her baby's spirit, the bent woman continued, or there will be no room for her to live.

The young girl appeared nervous with all this talk of the dead baby and spirits, because Navajos usually did not like to speak of these things. Bent Woman sensed this in her and became quiet.

Sam was grateful for the words of the old woman, but he did not understand how just knowing this could help his sister. "What can I do?" he asked, his words falling on the top of the bent woman's head.

"There is nothing for you to do," the old woman replied in English spoken with a Navajo rhythm. "Sad Woman must find her own vessel to house her baby's spirit."

Sam nodded understanding. He wiped the water that had fallen from his eyes with his chili-stained apron, and hoped that this thing would happen.

They must go now the young woman said, and thanked him once again for his kindness. As he watched them leave, Sam thought that he had never been paid so dearly for his humble chili.

He followed their progress down the road, the young girl was in the lead trailed by her mother. Bent Woman lagged behind, her feet surrounded by a cloud of dust. She stopped at a family of juniper trees and stared down at the ground. Sam looked beyond her and saw the stooped figure of his sister coming up the path. He noted the effort she took to make each step.

His sister walked to the figure of Bent Woman and looked down. On the ground was a baby morning dove lost from the protection of its mother. The two women waited some time to see if the mother was near. Then Sam's sister picked up the dove and nestled it in her hands. Bent Woman said something to her, then continued down the road her feet encircled in a fine cloud of dust. Sam's sister watched after her and then headed into the diner.

My mother would then tell me how Sam's sister cared for that little bird. How she poured her love into the bird, feeding it and keeping it warm. With her care the bird grew, and Sam's sister's heart became lighter and less constricted with grief. Sam thought that she was releasing her baby's spirit, and he watched with great happiness as the little bird and his sister grew stronger.

As time passed the little bird learned the coo of the dove, and how to make music with is wings when he flew. He made his home in the junipers and called other doves to him, and Fat Sam and his sister took much pleasure in their songs.

Sam's sister, now freed from the burden of her sorrow no longer walked hunched over. She had released her pain in the act of nurturing the bird, and felt alive again.

In the early morning times, Sam often hoped to see Bent Woman again, he wanted to thank her. For he was sure that she had worked some magic that day, that day of the little dove.

That is the story that my mother told me, the story that I have carried with me since childhood. And to this day, I cannot hear the coo of a morning dove without remembering the tale of Bent Woman and Fat Sam and the healing of his sister's heart.

THE BEAUTY SHOP

Here I sit in the shop of beauty, surrounded by
other hopefuls. Each of us surveying the other,
noting flaws, envying beauty. Convinced of our
inferiority. Pores too large, nose too big, skin
dull, dull, dull. Each hopeful to emerge this day
different than we appeared. Oh, fresh cut hair.
Oh, color new. Oh, never ending search for the girl that
we once knew.

YELLOW BOOTS

I went out to talk to the old man
across the street today.
It was early morning, after a night
of spring storms.
The air was fresh and clear, and
he stood tall, gaunt, sagging some,
wearing the pallor of age.

What drew me to him, simply
magnetized me, were his yellow
rain boots. They were the brightest
happiest boots that I had ever seen.
He wore them inconspicuously. Oblivious,
perhaps, to their dazzling effect.

We exchanged pleasantries - - both
grateful for the day. He, I think,
more so than I. He pointed then
to a bulge in his shirt at
his waist, and mumbled something
I could not quite catch.
I thought that he was trying to tell
me that he was sick, or the owner
of some growing mass.

I watched incredulously as he slowly
opened his shirt, and a small
duckling peered over his buttons
to share the morning light. It
had become separated from its
mother in the storm, and the
old man, now charged with its
care, was shielding it from harm.

The moral of this story should
be obviously clear - - if you
ever see an old man in yellow
boots, run to him as fast
as you can to see what
treasures he has to share.

THE RESERVATION

I sense the "old ones." Their presence
joined with this ancient land. Their
souls travel across the rugged terrain,
circling their children. No Navajo seems
ever alone, each person exists connected
to what was before. Navajo part earth,
earth part Navajo. I cannot separate
them from each other. I, a stranger, can
sense all this because they have allowed it.

ABERDEEN GULLS

What are the gulls crying about,
screaming about?
Gliding above seaside towns,
wings cutting through the air.
Is it some burden, unknown to us,
that is too difficult
for them to bear?

THE DREAM

Last night I dreamt that I was in my
grandfather's house. A country cottage
not seen for forty years.
I saw the rooms, felt the rooms, as the
person I am today, and with the recollection
of a child.

The cloudless images of the rooms connected
me to another time, fusing child and woman
and making me feel complete.

Preoccupied with the struggle of daily life
I had lost the memory of that time, and then
awoke with gratitude for the unencumbered
freedom of the dream.

THE NIGHT

I am thankful for the goodness
of the sweet night.
The night that covers fears and
cloaks worries.
The night whose hours stretch
endless, offering freedom from
the cares of daylight.

LOST

Sometimes we travel so far from ourselves
that we can barely find our way back.
We lose some sense of who we are somewhere
along the living highway and find ourselves
searching, in vain, for familiar signposts
or anything that would point the way and hasten our return.

FLIGHT

I am mesmerized by bodies in flight.
Anything that flies, or floats, or
drifts released from gravity's hold.
I am envious of their weightlessness,
their freedom from earthbound ties.
Oh, to fly, to dip and dive!
To ride on invisible currents and
break the chains that bind.

UNTITLED

Sometimes I read “my stuff” and I cannot
imagine who is on that page looking up
at me. Have you ever done that? Have
you ever caught a glimpse of yourself in
something you wrote and wondered where did
that come from? It is really amazing!
It is like a person leaves your head,
travels down your neck into your arm, then
into your fingers, then through the pen and
onto the page. What is even more amazing
is that it took man millions of years to
make that short journey.
There I go again. Now where did that come from?

SPECIAL THOUGHTS

HEALING

If I have found an outlet
for my moroseness it is
in the healing vehicle of
the poem.

Where feelings of child and woman
are announced across
the page and the lines
often reveal more of
myself than I would
normally care to know.

The wish to tell my story - -
if only to myself is
granted over and over again
by the curing rhythm of
the poem.

SPACE

Deep inside all of us
is a desire for space.
A yearning for openness.
A wish for a place
in which we do not collide
with the energies of others.

We live bruised and bruising,
marked by our encounters.

We long to stretch far beyond
our reach, and not be hampered
by the barrier of another soul.

BOYNTON CANYON

I arrive, laden with the burdens of city
life. The weight of them tethering me to
earth, binding my powers.

I hike, sheltered by the ponderosa pines.
My feet stumble on the trail, unaccustomed
to the freedom of the red dirt.

Drawn, as if by magic, to the canyon's mouth,
I sense release. My step lighter now, surer
now, carries me in to its vestibule.

Church-like stillness surrounds me, and the
sacredness of the red rock altars my
soul.

Anointed, I take my leave. Strong again.